MAX'S
BOX

Written by Brian Wray

Illustrated by Shiloh Penfield

Schiffer **Kids**™

4880 Lower Valley Road, Atglen, PA 19310

Other Schiffer Books by Brian Wray:
Unraveling Rose, ISBN: 978-0-7643-5393-2

Library of Congress Control Number: 2019936473

Edited by Kim Grandizio

Type set in Book Antinqua

ISBN: 978-0-7643-5804-3 (hard cover)
ISBN: 978-0-7643-5879-1 (soft cover)
Printed in China

Co-published by Pixel Mouse House & Schiffer Publishing, Ltd.
4880 Lower Valley Road
Atglen, PA 19310
Phone: (610) 593-1777; Fax: (610) 593-2002
E-mail: Info@schifferbooks.com
Web: www.schifferbooks.com

For our complete selection of fine books on this and related subjects, please visit our website at www.schifferbooks.com. You may also write for a free catalog.

Schiffer Publishing's titles are available at special discounts for bulk purchases for sales promotions or premiums. Special editions, including personalized covers, corporate imprints, and excerpts, can be created in large quantities for special needs. For more information, contact the publisher.

We are always looking for people to write books on new and related subjects. If you have an idea for a book, please contact us at proposals@schifferbooks.com.

For Nicole, Catherine, and Sylvia, who've given me more colorful balloons than I could ever hope to repay.

~ BW

For Will, my partner in crime.

~ SP

Max had a tiny box, small enough to fit into his little hand.

"This is yours," his mother told him.
"Everything will go into that Box," Father added.
"Small things, big things, all things."

And, he was right.

When Max put his favorite ball in the Box, the Box got bigger.

When he dropped his pirate ship in the Box, the Box got bigger.

And there was still enough room for Murphy the stuffed dog, and his lucky red truck. The little Box just kept growing.

When the Box became too large to carry, Max's parents bought him a wagon to pull the Box.

"Is that Box getting too big for you?" Father asked.
"I can carry it," Max insisted.

But Max learned that the Box didn't simply hold on to toys and stuffed dogs. This Box held on to Max's feelings, too.

When Max fell in the playground, an older boy told him, "Big boys don't cry." So Max put his hurt in the Box. And the Box grew.

Max became frustrated when he had trouble reading a story, and the other children teased him. So he put his anger in the Box, and the Box expanded right there beside him.

He was excited about the birthday party but felt too shy to make friends. Max hid his embarrassment in the Box, and the Box grew bigger still.

It didn't take long for the Box to outgrow the wagon…

And Max's big blue sled…

Even the family car.

Dragging around this huge Box was getting
harder-and-harder for Max.

Riding a bike was difficult.

Climbing trees with friends became impossible.

And swimming? Forget it. Still, he didn't feel he could let it go.

Before long,
Max couldn't
do anything
but sit in the
shadow of his
enormous Box.

He watched other children ride their bikes without a Box to hold them back, and felt all alone. Max was afraid that he was stuck with this great big Box forever.

That made Max even sadder.
And his Box grew.

One day, a boy passing by saw Max was upset, and stopped. Then the boy asked him a very important question.

"How are you feeling?"
"I'm feeling . . . sad," Max said nervously.
"I feel sad too sometimes," the boy told Max.
"Would you like to come to the park and play?"

Just then, a lady bug—bright red, big and round—landed on the Box, just above Max's head, and it gave him an idea. And the idea grew.

Slipping a piece of chalk from his pocket, he drew a squiggly line, so that the lady bug looked like a baby balloon floating away.

That bug's bright red looked so beautiful that it made Max smile, and Max's smile made the Box lighter somehow.

"This feels better," Max said to his new friend.
The boy asked, "Can I make a balloon, too?"
"Sure," said Max, happy to share.

The boy drew a big green balloon. Then a little girl drew an even bigger purple and yellow one. With each balloon, Max began to forget about what was in the Box.

People on the way home from work, or school, or the store stopped to draw balloons of their own.

It was really something to see, this giant Box with brilliant balloons.

Even Mother and Father drew a great big bunch.

There were so many balloons, in fact, that something wonderful happened. The Box began to float! High enough that the rope around Max's wrist tugged, pulling him to his tip-toes.

Max loved seeing those beautiful colors dancing in the clear blue sky.

But Max was so used to holding on to that great big Box and everything inside — toys, feelings, worries — that Max wasn't sure who he'd be without the Box.

"It's ok to have all kinds of feelings," Father whispered. "But once you feel them, their job is done."

And so, Max let it go.

Everyone watched as the rainbow of balloons drifted across the sky, and they felt just a little bit brighter . . . and a little bit lighter.

Especially Max.

A word about Emotions

Learning to express emotion is one of the main ingredients of a child's healthy emotional and social development. Still, navigating powerful emotions can be a challenge—not only for the child, but for their parents and caregivers.

During emotional episodes, well-meaning adults may try to "fix" the source of the upset, to make the negative emotions go away. Other times, they may try to distract the child from what they're feeling by drawing their attention elsewhere. Whatever the strategy, children begin to sense that there is something wrong in recognizing and expressing their emotions, and learn to suppress them.

Suppressing negative feelings, however, can lead to multiple problems; even jeopardizing their basic ability to function. Learning to "stuff down" emotions early in life can lead to feeling isolated as they grow older, potentially causing anxiety and depression.

Further, lingering stereotypes about gender behavior still influence expectations of how children should express their emotions. However, research has shown that up to the age of five, boys are more likely to express their feelings than girls.

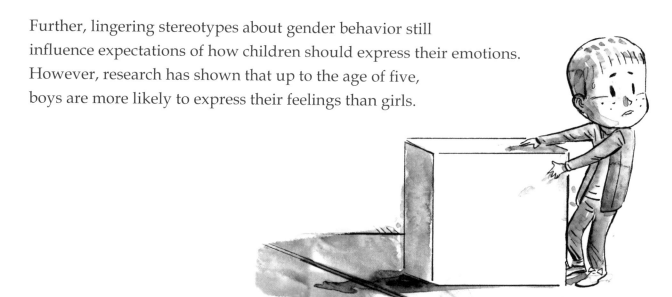

Here are a few ways that adults can help a child express and manage their emotions in a healthy way:

- An adult's impulse to "fix" whatever is causing the negative feelings is understandable. Simply showing a child that you want to understand what they're saying can be a more effective way of helping them manage the situation. Try asking, "How are you feeling?" or saying, "I see you're upset right now."

- Boys, research shows, are more prone to releasing feelings in physical outbursts. Rather than trying to talk about emotions in the middle of an episode, wait to discuss it. Give them time to settle down, then try having a talk with them about what happened.

- Emotions can feel overwhelming to children. They're still learning that what they're feeling will eventually pass. Help a child manage their emotions by teaching them coping strategies. Repeating phrases like "I can do it," taking deep breaths, or spending time away from the situation are just three ways that can help a child reduce feeling frustrated and overwhelmed.

- Well-intentioned adults can indirectly convey that there is something wrong with crying. Let children know that crying is okay. Sadness, fear, pain, anger, and even happiness can be accompanied by tears. Acknowledge the emotion that is motivating the tears, rather than the crying itself.

- Creating an open environment that allows children to express their emotions enables them to understand and identify not only their own feelings, but also the feelings of others.

Brian was born in Cincinnati, Ohio, and moved to New York after graduating from Penn State. In 2003, Brian was awarded the Nicholl Fellowship in Screenwriting. He writes from Brooklyn, where he lives with his wife, two daughters, and their endless inspiration. Brian is also the author of *Unraveling Rose*, the 2017 Foreword INDIES Gold Winner for "Picture Books, Early Reader."

Shiloh's previous works include the children's book *Unraveling Rose*, *Boy Zero Comic*, a guest artist spot on *Red Knight* comic, and multiple independent projects. Located in Brooklyn, her calico cat "Maki" maintains quality control and ensures all pages are delivered on time.